NORMAN BRIDWELL

Clifford's
ABC

scarecrow

elephant

dog

elf

ISBN 978-1-338-05356-2

Printed in China 38

Style: 978-1-338-05356-2
Factory Number: 123386
4/16 - 9/16

This special edition was printed for Kohl's Department Stores, Inc.
(for distribution on behalf of Kohl's Cares, LLC, its wholly owned subsidiary)
by Scholastic Inc.

NORMAN BRIDWELL
Clifford's
ABC

alligator

beaver

cow

SCHOLASTIC INC.

Aa
accordion
acorns
alligator
anchor
ant
anvil
armadillo
axe

Aa

accordion

axe

armadillo

anvil

acorns

alligator

ant

anchor

Bb

bird

ball

bat

boots

beaver

basket

balloon

boy

boat

butterfly

bottle

baby

Cc

Cc
cactus
cake
candle
cape
cat
checks
clown
collar
cook
cow

collar

cow

cat

cook

candle

cake

cactus

cape

clown

checks

Dd

dragon

dolphin

dog

dummy

drum

derby

dandelion

Ee
eagle
earring
eel
egg
elephant
elf
Eskimo

eagle

egg

Ee

earring

elephant

eel

Eskimo

elf

Ff

flag

frog

fly

fish

fire

fairy

flea

funnel

flower

fox

ghost

gorilla

giraffe

garden

goat

glove

garbage can

G g

Hh

helicopter

harp

house

horse

hollyhock

hummingbird

hat

horn

haystack

hippopotamus

Ii

Ii
ice cream cone
igloo
iguana
ink
iris
iron

iguana

igloo

iris

ink

ice cream cone

iron

Jj

jet

juggler

jogger

jack-o'-lantern

jester

jacks

Kk

kangaroo
karate
kayak
kitten
knight
knitting
koala

Ll

lamb
lasso
leopard
lily
lion
lobster
log
lumberjack

K k

L l

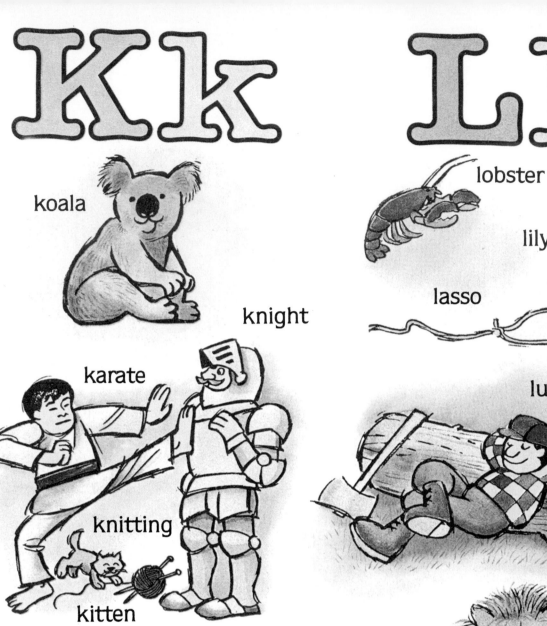

koala

lobster

lily

lasso

knight

karate

knitting

kitten

lumberjack

log

kangaroo

kayak

leopard

lamb

lion

Mm

moon

mop

map

mask

monkey

mittens

mouse

marionette

magician

magnet

M

Nn

Nn
nest
net
noodles
note
nun
nurse
nut
nutcracker

note

nest

net

nun

nutcracker

nut

nurse

noodles

Oo

owl

orchid

ostrich

octopus

orange

overalls

oar

Pp
paintbrush
palette
palm
panda
parachute
pear
picture
pig
pineapple
pirate
pony
porcupine

parachute

palm

pineapple

panda

picture

pirate

pear

palette

pony

pig

porcupine

Qq

quail

quartet

question

queen

quilt

Rr
rabbit
raccoon
racket
radishes
rain
rainbow
rake
rhinoceros
robot
rocket
roller skate
rope
rug

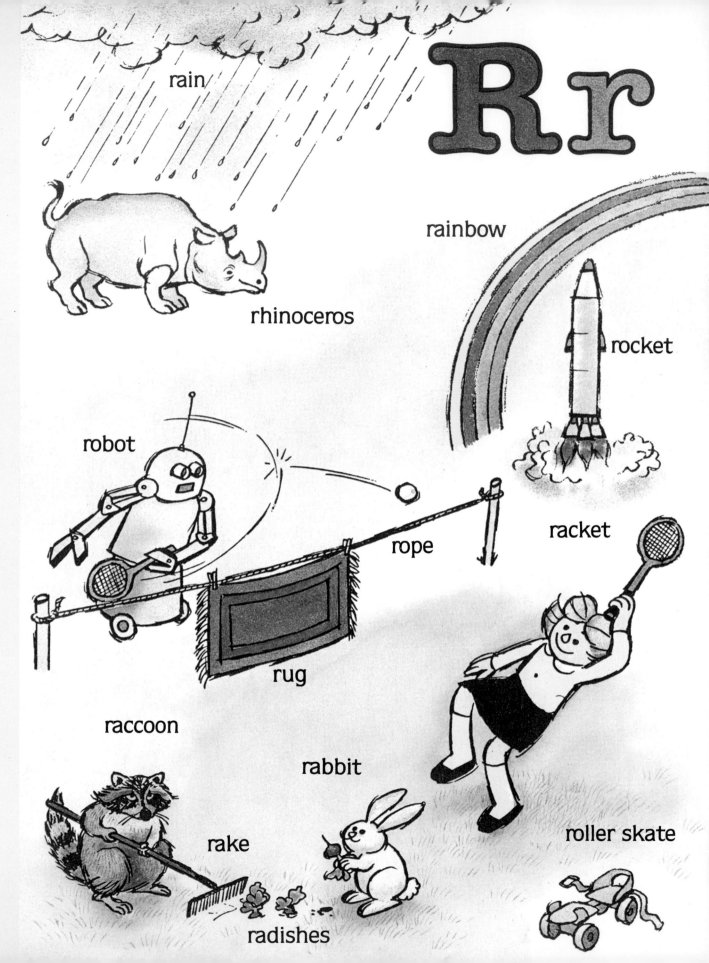

rain

Rr

rainbow

rhinoceros

rocket

robot

rope

racket

rug

raccoon

rabbit

roller skate

rake

radishes

Ss

Saturn

star

scarecrow

sleep

saxophone

soccer ball

sausage

seesaw

sandwich

squirrel

snail

seal

stool

Tt

Tt
table
teapot
teddy bear
telescope
television
tent
tepee
tiger
tractor
train
turtle

tepee

tent

tractor

tiger

telescope

television

teapot

train

teddy bear

turtle

table

Uu

umbrella

UFO

unicorn

umpire

urn

ukulele

unicycle

Vv

volcano

vampire

valentine

violets

vise

violin

vacuum cleaner

vase

Vv
vacuum cleaner
valentine
vampire
vase
violets
violin
vise
volcano

Ww

whale

waves

walrus

wrenches

wheelbarrow

witch

wolf

worm

waffles

wagon

W

Xx Yy

xylophone

yacht

x-ray

yak

yawn

yarn

yo-yo

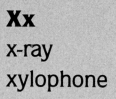

Xx
x-ray
xylophone

Yy
yacht
yak
yarn
yawn
yo-yo

zeppelin

Zz

zebra

zipper

zither

ZOO

Z